Just George

The favourite character from

Enid Blyton's
Famous Five

George, Timmy and the Haunted Cave

*The **Just George** series*
by Sue Welford

Just George

The favourite character from

Enid Blyton's

Famous Five

George, Timmy and the Haunted Cave

Sue Welford

Illustrated by Lesley Harker

*Hodder
Children's
Books*

a division of Hodder Headline Limited

First published in Great Britain in 2000
by Hodder Children's Books

10 9 8 7 6 5 4 3 2

For further information on Enid Blyton,
please contact www.blyton.com

A Catalogue record for this book is available from
the British Library.

ISBN 0 340 77863 6

Typeset by Avon Dataset Ltd, Bidford-on-Avon, Warks

Printed and bound in Great Britain by
The Guernsey Press Co. Ltd, Channel Isles

Hodder Children's Books
A division of Hodder Headline Limited
338 Euston Road
London NW1 3BH

Contents

1

A new friend

'Georgina! What *have* you done?' cried George's mother, staring at her in horror.

'I've cut my hair,' said George, standing in front of the mirror in the kitchen. 'It was growing all around my neck and I hated it.'

'But you look just like a boy!' said her mother, gazing at George's short, dark curls then at the

rest of her hair lying in a little heap on the floor.

'Good,' said George. 'That's exactly what I *want* to look like.' She threw down the scissors. 'I'm going to get on with building my tree-house now.'

'Boys' haircuts, tree-houses, whatever next!' George heard her poor mother sigh as she went out of the back door, slamming it shut behind her.

George went into the garden shed to fetch the hammer and nails and was soon hammering and banging up in the tall old apple tree in the garden. In fact, she was making so much noise that it wasn't long before her father came charging out of his study.

'What *is* that dreadful noise?' he shouted with an angry look on his face. 'How on earth am I supposed to do any work with that racket going on?'

George's father was very tall, very dark and had an extraordinary-looking face with a wide forehead and fierce, dark brows. He frowned an awful lot, just like George.

'It's all right, Quentin,' said George's mother, trying to calm her husband down. 'It's only Georgina. She's building a tree-house.'

'Well, go and tell her to build it somewhere else,' said her husband. 'She's disturbing my studies. What's the point of living in a quiet house by the sea if people go hammering and banging all the time?'

George's father was a scientist. He spent hours in his study working out difficult scientific problems and became very bad-tempered when he was disturbed.

George and her mother and father lived in a large, three hundred-year-old, white-stone house on top of a small cliff overlooking the sea.

The house was called Kirrin Cottage even though it was too big to really be a cottage. It had red roses growing round the old wooden front door and a garden full of flowers. The house had been in her mother's family for many years and she wouldn't dream of living anywhere else. George loved to sit upstairs in one of the rooms that overlooked the sea and dream of smugglers and storms and shipwrecks and all the exciting things that had happened years ago and might even happen again one day.

Below the cliff was Kirrin Bay. The bay was beautiful, with a wide sweep of yellow sand and a dear little rocky island guarding the entrance. On a small hill in the centre of Kirrin Island was a wonderful, mysterious ruined castle that had once stood proud and strong, looking out to sea. George's favourite thing in all the world was playing in the castle's two tumbledown towers or inside the ruined room across the stone courtyard where a huge old fireplace was built into one of the walls. She could get to the island by rowing her little wooden dinghy carefully through a reef of dangerous rocks, landing eventually on the golden sand of the little island cove. She loved the rabbits and sea birds that lived on the island and thought that the castle was the most eerie and exciting place she had ever seen in her life.

After her father's angry outburst about the terrible noise that George was making with her hammer, her mother gave a sigh and went outside to find her.

'Hello, Mummy,' said George, staring down from the tree with her brilliant blue eyes. She had nailed two planks together across the branches and was just about to nail another one to them. 'This is going to be such fun when I've finished it, don't you think?'

'I'm afraid you've got to come down, Georgina,' said her mother firmly. 'Father's busy and you're disturbing him.'

George jumped down from the tree with a scowl on her face. 'Oh, Mummy, *please* don't call me Georgina. You know I hate it. Call me George.'

'Your name is Georgina,' insisted her mother. 'George is a boy's name.'

'I know,' said George, standing with her hands on her hips. 'That's why I like it. Most of all in the world I'd like to be a boy, so if you call me Georgina I shan't answer.'

'Oh, dear,' sighed her mother. 'Why can't you just be content to be a girl?'

'I don't know,' said George, screwing up her freckled nose. 'I just know that I hate doing things that girls do. Dressing in frilly frocks, playing with dolls and having pretend tea parties.' She pulled a face. 'Ugh, I hate them! I like climbing and swimming and running and sailing *and* I can do all those as good as any boy, so there.'

'And building tree-houses,' said her mother with a smile.

'Exactly,' said George, still scowling fiercely. 'Girls' games make me sick and I won't play them for anything.'

Her mother sighed again. 'Well, I wish you would make friends with some of the girls in Kirrin village. It would be lovely for you to have

7

someone to play with. I thought about asking your cousins to stay for the holidays but Father said four children in the house would make too much noise.'

George's cousins lived in London. Their names were Julian, Dick and Anne but George had never met them. She didn't particularly want to, especially as one of them was a girl!

George scowled even harder at the thought of her cousins coming to stay at Kirrin Cottage. 'I don't want anyone to play with, Mummy,' she insisted. 'And I don't want any other children staying here. I *like* being on my own.'

'Oh, well, Georgina,' said her mother. 'It's up to you, I suppose. But you'll have to find something else to do for now, I'm afraid.'

Because her mother had called her 'Georgina', the little girl ignored her. She stood there with her hands in the pockets of her shorts, whistling and looking up at the sky in a very boyish fashion.

'Georgina, *George*. Did you hear what I said?' asked her mother in an exasperated voice.

'Yes,' said George. 'And I haven't any idea what I'm going to do now. I *was* having a lovely time and now Father has spoiled it.'

'You can finish your tree-house later when Father has finished his work,' said her mother.

'But Father has *never* finished work,' complained George. 'And even if he *thinks* he's finished then he quickly remembers he hasn't.'

George's mother sighed for the third time in a very short while. George was right about her father. When he was busy, which was almost always, he even forgot what day it was, and if he didn't draw the study curtains back he wouldn't know whether it was morning, noon or night. He was so wrapped up in his work that he would often leap up in the middle of dinner to go and finish a problem they had thought he'd already solved. He spent hours in his study working on important scientific formulas and writing books about them. He often stayed there for days on end.

She patted George's short curls. 'Well, why don't you go up on the moor, darling?' she suggested. 'It's a lovely day, just right for a walk.'

'Oh, all right,' said George sulkily. She strode off through the gate at the end of the garden leaving her poor mother to put away the hammer and nails.

George climbed the steep path to the moor. She forgot that she was angry as she looked up at the vivid blue sky and the lazy cotton-wool clouds drifting by. She could hear a skylark singing in the distance and the smell of the heather blew towards her on the breeze. It was *much* too nice a day to be annoyed for very long! In fact, George was the kind of person who flared up easily but never stayed angry for long. She could be rude and haughty and very fierce at times but she was a very loving and loyal and extremely honest little girl.

George put her hands her pockets and strode along, whistling as well as any boy could. 'Girls' games,' she muttered to herself. 'I *hate* girls and I don't need anyone to play with. I'm all right as I am, thank you, Mummy dear!'

Soon, she was a long way away from Kirrin Cottage, high up on the moor with gorse and heather as far as she could see and the sound of the sea breaking against the base of the cliffs far below. She was all alone, just as she liked to be.

On that particular day, though, George was not going to be alone for very long. What she did not know was that very soon she was going to find a friend. Someone who would be the best friend anyone could ever have in the whole world. Even George!

2

A discovery

George was bowling along quite merrily when a most peculiar noise stopped her in her tracks. It was a kind of whining, squeaking noise and it came from a clump of undergrowth by the side of the path.

She frowned. What on earth was it? Could it be a wild animal of some kind? A rabbit or a badger perhaps? George's curiosity got the better of her and she bent down to have a look.

'Oh!' exclaimed the little girl. There, sitting under a gorse bush, was a tiny puppy. George let out of a cry of astonishment and stretched out her hand. She grasped the puppy gently by the scruff of its neck and drew it towards her and up into her arms. 'Oh, you poor dear little thing!' she cried, holding the puppy against her and stroking its fluffy head. 'Where on earth did you come from?' She looked around but there was not a soul in sight. How on earth did the little creature come to be out on the moors, she wondered, all alone just like her?

George sat down with the puppy on her lap. He was a kind of sandy brown colour with scruffy fur and a very long tail. He had a little round black nose and huge, melting, brown eyes. As she stroked him, the puppy gave a little whine as if to say 'thank you for finding me' and licked her freckled nose and cheeks with his rough, pink tongue.

'Oh, you're so sweet,' said George. 'Where are your mummy and daddy?'

But there was no answer to her questions, only another little whine from the puppy. He snuggled down on her lap, happy not to be alone any longer.

George just did not know what to do. If she carried him back to Kirrin Cottage and the puppy's owners were somewhere around they would not be very pleased to return and find him gone. But then if they *were* around and they had left the puppy to play by himself then they did not deserve to have him. George suddenly began to feel very angry indeed. What kind of a horrid person would leave such a young animal all by itself?

Making up her mind what to do at last, George stood up with the puppy in her arms and began to walk all the way back home to Kirrin Cottage. She would ask her parents. *They* would know what to do!

After a little while, George's arms grew tired of carrying the puppy so she put him down on the path. He scampered along beside her, full of energy and so pleased to have been rescued by someone as nice and kind as this little girl. He had been very happy snuggled in her warm arms but now it was lovely to be springing along by her side.

The puppy gave little yapping sounds and ran after a stick that George threw for him. Soon they were having a fine old game.

'Puppy! Puppy!' called George as the little dog ran off into the heather, then came bouncing back towards her. What fun he was to play with!

When she came to her gate, George picked the puppy up again and ran up the garden path and in through the back door. The woman who helped in the house was in the kitchen making some scones for tea.

'Joanna, look who I've found!' cried George as she hurtled in.

'Oh!' squealed Joanna as she saw what George carried in her arms. 'Where on earth did it come from?'

George explained that she had found the puppy high up on the moor.

'Goodness me,' said Joanna. 'Who would leave such a sweet little creature on its own so far from home?'

'I've no idea,' said George. 'Someone perfectly horrid obviously. Whoever it was, they deserve to be punished. It's a very cruel thing to do, don't you think, Joanna?'

'I certainly do,' said Joanna. She went to the fridge and took out a bottle of milk. She poured some into a saucer and put it on the floor. 'Here you are, Poppet,' she said to the puppy. 'Let's see if you're thirsty.'

'Do dogs drink milk?' asked George who had never had a dog and did not really know anything about them.

'Yes, of course,' said Joanna. 'He's only a baby and all babies drink milk.'

They both watched as the puppy lapped hungrily.

'What kind of a dog do you think he is?' asked George.

'I've no idea,' answered Joanna. 'His head looks too big, his ears too pricked and his tail altogether too long. It's impossible to tell.'

'Well, I don't really care what kind of a dog he is,' remarked George. 'I think he's simply wonderful.'

'Who's wonderful?' asked her mother coming through the door.

'This puppy,' said George.

'*Puppy*!' exclaimed Mother. Then she saw what George meant. 'Oh, my goodness, Georgina. Whose is it?'

George was too thrilled about finding the puppy to notice her mother had called her Georgina. When her mother asked her who the puppy belonged to she wanted to say 'me' but she knew he wasn't really hers. Things didn't belong to you just because you had found them. She explained what had happened.

'Well, the best thing you can do,' said her mother, 'is to take him to the village and ask if anyone has lost a puppy. He may have wandered on to the moor all by himself.'

'All right, Mummy,' said George, pulling a sad little face. 'I suppose I'd better.'

When the puppy had finished his milk he ran over to George and growled and began to play with the laces of her plimsolls. George and her mother and Joanna thought that was very funny and all laughed loudly. So loudly, in fact, that

Father came out of his study to see what the joke was all about.

'What's this!' he exclaimed when he saw the little dog.

'A puppy, Father,' said George.

'I can see *that*, Georgina,' said the tall man in a stern voice. 'I *mean* what is it doing here?'

Again, George did not protest about being called Georgina. She didn't want Father to be angry about her bringing the puppy home. She decided she had better keep in his good books. Sometimes George couldn't control her temper and would give hot answers to people without thinking. This time she just softly and sensibly explained all over again about finding the puppy.

To George's relief, her father was not angry at all. He bent and stroked the puppy. 'My word, he's a nice little fellow, isn't he?' he said as the puppy licked his hand. 'Someone will be very upset that they've lost him.'

'You'd better take him to the village now,' said Mother to George. 'You could try the police station too, to find out if anyone has reported a lost dog.'

'Very well,' sighed George. She picked the puppy up and went out feeling very sad. Having a dog would be such fun. In fact, it would be the best friend anyone could ever have. Wouldn't it be wonderful if no-one knew who he belonged to and she was allowed to keep him for ever.

To get from Kirrin Cottage to the village, George had to walk past the little harbour where the fishermen kept their boats. As she walked by, Alf, a fisherman's son, called out to her. He could see she was carrying a puppy and wondered if it belonged to her.

'Got a new puppy, George?' he called from where he was sitting on the edge of a boat mending a fishing net. He had met George several times before and knew she did not like being called by her proper name.

George walked down the steps towards him. 'I found him.'

'Found him?' cried Alf as he stroked the little dog and generally made a fuss of him. 'Where?'

Alf looked amazed when George told him. 'I suppose you don't know anyone who has lost a puppy, do you?' she asked, half-hoping he would say no.

Alf shook his head. 'No, no-one. It's very strange that he should be up on the moor all by himself, poor little tyke.' He stroked the puppy again. 'He's lovely.'

'Yes,' sighed George and went on her way. The puppy struggled in her arms so she put him down and he trotted beside her, looking up at her now and then as if to make sure she was still there. He had been lost once and didn't want to get lost again. In fact, he felt so safe and secure with this little girl he would like to stay with her all the time from now on.

Just as George and the puppy were about to cross the sleepy high street a very large motorbike roared past.

'Careful!' cried George, scooping the puppy up into her arms as he very nearly stepped into its path. 'What horrid person is riding so fast through the village?' said George with a frown. Kirrin was usually very quiet with a general absence of noisy traffic and that was just the way George liked it.

'Wuff,' barked the puppy as if to say he didn't know, but he thought they were horrid too.

George crossed the street and went into the post office. The post office was part of the village store which sold everything from tintacks to tinned tomatoes.

The post mistress, Mrs Wood, was behind the counter. She was very short and rather plump and sat on a high stool. In fact, the stool was so high her feet dangled quite a long way from the floor.

Mrs Wood had a parrot in a cage hanging from

the ceiling and it imitated the sound of the doorbell clanging as George and the puppy came through. *Ding dong, ding dong!* It was difficult to tell which was the real bell and which was the parrot.

'Who is it?' the parrot said as George went towards the counter. She chuckled. Mrs Wood's parrot always made her laugh. 'Who is it?' repeated the parrot loudly.

'Do be quiet, Polly,' said Mrs Wood. 'Can't you see it's the young lady from Kirrin Cottage?'

George winced. Being called a young lady was even worse than being called Georgina!

'Young lady,' said Polly. 'Young lady. *Ding dong.*'

George could not help grinning as she picked up the puppy to show Mrs Wood. 'You don't know who he belongs to, do you?' she asked.

'Oh, what a sweet little creature,' exclaimed Mrs Wood. 'Where *did* you find him?'

By the time George had walked all round the village it seemed she had explained a dozen or more times where she had found the puppy. But no-one had lost him. No-one knew where he came from. She stopped one or two people in the street and asked them but none of them knew anything about a puppy. A tall man wearing a dark leather jacket ignored her and pushed past rudely when she tried to approach him.

'Rude man!' George muttered as she made her way along to the police station to ask if anyone had reported a lost dog.

PC Moon looked over the counter at the puppy, then opened a big blue covered book he kept beside him. In the book he kept a note of things that had been lost and found.

After he had looked through several pages, the policeman shook his head. 'Sorry, Miss, no-one's reported a missing puppy.'

'Well, what should I do with him, then?' asked George, scowling a little because the policeman had called her 'miss'.

'Well,' said PC Moon. 'If no-one claims him within thirty days then you can keep him, if your parents agree.'

'Thirty days!' exclaimed George. 'That's ages and ages, the school holidays will almost be over by then.'

'Well,' said PC Moon. 'Those are the rules. Do you want me to phone the dog rescue centre? They'll keep him for that time if you like.'

George hugged the puppy close. She could not bear to think of letting him go. He snuggled against her and licked her hand as if to say 'please keep me for ever and ever'. Then George had an idea. She would ask her mother and father if *she* could keep the dog for the thirty days. She knew he would be much happier at Kirrin Cottage than at the dog rescue centre. He could help her finish the tree-house. She could take him for wonderful walks on the beach and row him over to the island where they could play games in the castle. She could even take him to climb on the rocks where a giant shipwreck lay just below the surface of the water. The ship had once belonged to George's great, great grandfather and had lain there for years and years. She knew the puppy would absolutely love it. The people at the rescue centre would be very kind to him but there would be lots of other dogs there and no-one would have the time to cuddle him or take him on adventures.

'I'll ask my parents if I can keep him until the

time is up,' George said to the police officer. 'If they say yes I'll telephone you to let you know.'

'Right you are, Miss,' said PC Moon when he had written down all the details of where George had found the puppy and a description of what the little dog looked like. 'You give me a ring when you get home and let me know what your parents say. If they say yes and anyone comes in who's lost a puppy I'll send them over to Kirrin Cottage.'

'Thanks very much,' said George. She scooped the puppy up in her arms and went out.

On the way home she passed Alf again. 'Any luck?' he called.

She explained to him what the constable had said.

'What will happen if no-one claims him?' asked Alf.

'Well,' said George with a merry twinkle in her eye because she couldn't help feeling excited and thrilled at the thought of having a dog. 'I'm hoping that Mummy and Father will love him so much they'll want him to stay at Kirrin Cottage for ever!'

Alf grinned. 'Let's keep our fingers crossed then, shall we?'

'You bet,' called George as she waved goodbye to Alf and set off, whistling, towards home once more.

At Kirrin Cottage, George's mother was in the garden tending her flowers and vegetables. She listened carefully as George told her what had happened in the village. George put the puppy down and he scampered off towards the vegetable patch, poking his little black nose in between the rows of carrots and onions and beans as if he was exploring an exciting jungle.

'So, please, Mummy,' said George when she had finished explaining, 'please can we keep him here until someone claims him?'

Mother gazed at George, then at the puppy who by now was quite happily chewing one of the beansticks.

George held her breath. Would Mummy say yes or no? If the answer was yes she would be the happiest, most contented little girl in the whole wide world!

3

A special meal

In the garden at Kirrin Cottage, George's mother was looking thoughtful. She wasn't at all sure it was a good idea for George to keep the puppy she had found on the moor.

'Please, Mummy,' said George once more. 'I know he'll be ever so good and I promise to keep him quiet when Father's working.'

Her mother sighed. 'Well, all I can do is ask your father,' she said, smiling suddenly. 'If *he* thinks it's a good idea then I do too.'

George was suddenly filled with happiness. She threw her arms round her mother's waist and gave her a big hug. 'Oh, thank you, Mummy! When will you ask him?'

'When he's in a good mood,' said her mother, hugging George back. 'You know there's always a right time and a wrong time with Father. You'll have to try to be patient.'

But being patient was not one of the things that George did best. She wanted to know if the puppy could stay at Kirrin Cottage until his owner was found. She could not possibly wait until Father was in a good mood to ask him. It could be ages and ages before that happened. In fact, he *had* been known to be in a bad mood for the whole of the school holidays with George not seeing him smile once.

Then she had a bright idea. 'If Joanna cooks him his favourite dinner *that* will make him in a good mood,' she said.

Her mother laughed. 'That's a very good idea,

Georgina, er, George. Why don't you go and ask her?'

George skipped indoors with the puppy trotting beside her. He really was the sweetest little creature you could ever see. He was so keen on staying as close to the little girl as possible, it seemed as if he was attached to her feet by a piece of string.

As George opened the back door the puppy rushed in front of her, slipping and sliding on the polished tiled floor of the hall and skidding into the kitchen. He came to a halt beside Joanna's feet just as she was trying to decide what to cook for dinner that evening.

'Are you still here?' said Joanna, bending to stroke the puppy. She looked up at George. 'You didn't manage to find out who owns him, then?'

George shook her head. 'No.' She went on to explain what PC Moon had told her about keeping the puppy for thirty days in case an owner showed up.

'And PC Moon said I could keep him here if Mummy and Father agreed and I *do* so want to,' she said breathlessly. 'And Mummy's going to ask

Father so will you please cook his favourite dinner to put him in a good mood?'

Joanna smiled at the little girl's eager face with her dark curls bouncing above her vivid blue eyes. 'Well,' she said. 'Your mother bought some fresh salmon yesterday so we'll have that with new potatoes and salad. That's one of your father's favourite meals so I'll do that tonight, shall I?'

George grinned. 'Oh, yes please! And how about apple crumble and custard for pudding? You know he likes that too.'

'Very well,' said Joanna. 'But you'll have to go out into the orchard and pick me some cooking apples.'

'Oh, I will,' said George. She bent down and picked up the puppy. He had been growling and tearing at the rug in front of the stove, gripping the corner between his sharp little puppy teeth and shaking it to and fro. 'Do you hear that, Puppy? Salmon and new potatoes! If *that* doesn't put Father in a good temper then nothing will!'

The puppy looked at George with his little head

cocked to one side. Then he stuck out his long pink tongue and licked her nose. Salmon and new potatoes sounded a *very* good idea indeed!

'I do believe that dog understands every word you're saying,' remarked Joanna as she went to the fridge to fetch the salmon.

'Of course he does,' said George. 'He's the most beautiful, clever dog in the whole, wide world!'

'I had a dog when I was your age,' said Joanna as she bustled about preparing the meal. 'Now he *was* the most lively and bright dog you could ever meet. He was wonderful and I loved him with all my heart.'

George sat on the floor playing with the puppy. He kept growling and pretending to bite her fingers. 'What was your dog's name?' she asked Joanna, looking up at her.

'Timothy,' said Joanna dreamily. 'He was brave and loyal and he went everywhere with me. People used to say he was like my little shadow.'

'Timothy,' murmured George thoughtfully. 'That's a jolly good name for a loyal and clever dog. I shall call *this* little dog Timothy too. It suits him very well, don't you think?'

'It certainly does,' said Joanna gazing at the puppy with a smile on her round face.

George stood up. 'Right, that's decided, then. Come on, Timothy, let's go and pick some apples for Father's favourite pudding.'

Together, George and Timothy ran outside, down the garden and into the little orchard at the far end.

'Stay here,' she said to Timothy, pushing down gently on his back so he sat down by the tree-trunk. 'I shan't be a minute so don't try to follow me. Dogs can't climb trees, you know.'

Timothy watched as George climbed the tree as fast as a monkey. When he saw her balancing on a dangerous-looking branch he gave a worried yelp and tried to jump up the trunk after her, bouncing up and down like a yo-yo.

George looked down at him and giggled. She felt sure Timothy *would* have climbed up after her if he had been able. She stuffed all her pockets full of apples and soon clambered down again.

'Good boy, Tim,' she said, bending down and giving him a cuddle before the two of them ran back indoors.

'Here you are, Joanna,' said George, tipping the shiny green apples from her pockets on to the table. 'Now we're going to find Father and tell him what's for dinner.'

Joanna picked up one of the apples and held it to her nose. 'Mmm, lovely,' she said. 'This apple smells of summer.'

George took one and sniffed it. 'So it does.' She put it to Timothy's nose so he could sniff it too.

'Wurf,' he said, making a sound in between a yap and a bark.

George and Joanna laughed.

'Now, I don't think you should bother your father for the moment,' the housekeeper said. 'He's very busy. Why don't you take Timmy out while I prepare these apples and get the rest of the meal ready. I'm sure the little fellow would love a walk.'

George suddenly remembered they didn't have any puppy food. What on earth was Timothy going to have for *his* dinner?

'Oh, dear. I don't know,' said Joanna when George asked her. 'You'd better go and ask your mother.'

So George ran back outside to find her. She was in the front garden now, tending the rambling rose that grew around the front door of the cottage. Timothy bounced beside George as she ran. He rather liked all this hurrying to and fro. It got rid of his puppy energy.

The first thing George told her mother was that she had decided on a name for the puppy.

'That's very nice,' said Mother. 'You can call him Timmy for short.' She was smiling but she also looked rather worried. 'You mustn't get too fond of him, dear. Supposing Father doesn't . . .'

But George didn't want to hear what would happen if her father wouldn't let Timothy stay at Kirrin Cottage for a while. She was very good at not listening to things she didn't want to hear so she just interrupted her mother and said, 'Please may I go to the village and buy some puppy food for Timmy? He's very hungry.'

'Yap, yap,' said Timothy, agreeing with her. He sat down on her left foot with his tail wagging nineteen to the dozen. 'Wurf, wurf,' he barked, trying to sound like a very hungry grown-up dog rather than a puppy.

George's mother could not help smiling. She reached into her coat pocket and took out her purse. She handed George a five pound note. 'Take this to the pet shop and buy some puppy food. And you'd better hurry, they'll be closing soon.'

George's eyes shone. 'Thanks, Mummy.' She patted her leg. 'Come on, Timmy, good boy.'

The little dog followed George through the gate and on to the path that led to the village. He was so happy to be near her he trotted along beside her as good as gold. He had forgotten all about the loneliness and fear he had felt when he was up on the moor. Things were certainly looking up. He had a new name, a new mistress, and a lovely new house close to the sea. Life, Timothy decided, was very good indeed.

4

Father makes a decision

George and Timothy trotted along as if they had been friends for ever. George chatted away. Although she hadn't minded being alone before, she had to admit it was lovely to have someone to talk to. It was late afternoon and the sky had a rosy glow as the sun got ready to go down. Every now and then Timothy spotted something that caught his puppy attention.

Once, he dived into the hedgerow and came out with a stick. He laid it at George's feet.

'Timmy, you're so clever!' cried George, picking up the stick and throwing it. Timothy leapt after it, picked it up and trotted back to George.

George suddenly realized the shops really would be closing if they didn't hurry. She picked Timothy up, tucked him under her arm and hurried on towards the village.

At the little harbour she stopped and looked out over the sea. It was a warm, shimmering blue. Round the corner of the jutting cliff she could just see Kirrin Island and the ruined castle tower.

'See that, Timmy,' said George, holding the puppy up so he could get a better view, 'that island is going to belong to me one day. If Father lets you stay with me I'll take you there in my little boat. But you have to promise not to chase the rabbits or birds.'

Timothy looked up at her. 'Wuff,' he said solemnly, promising he would do no such thing.

George gave him a squeeze. 'We can have lots

of adventures,' she said. 'It's the best place in the world.'

Timmy looked at the island with his little ears pricked up as high as they would go. It certainly *did* look a very exciting place indeed. He was not quite sure, though, that he liked the look of the great waves breaking against the rocks that seemed to go right round the island. They looked a bit dangerous to his puppy eyes!

By the time George and Timothy returned home, dinner was almost ready. As they came through the back door carrying a large bag of puppy food, Joanna was just dishing up the delicious-looking new potatoes.

'Please may we have a bowl for Timmy?' asked George as she dumped the bag of dog food on to the table. Timothy sat down at her feet staring hopefully up at the table. His little stomach had been rumbling for hours. He gave several little yaps and yelps and tried to jump up to grab the bag.

'Down, Timothy!' George commanded sternly. Straightaway Timothy sat down to wait patiently while she found a bowl and tipped some food into it. She placed it on the floor with a bowl of clean water beside it. Immediately the little dog dived towards the bowl, gobbling up the food as if it might disappear if he didn't.

'My goodness,' said Joanna. 'He's got an appetite!'

George watched as Timothy licked the last remnants of the food from the bowl. 'He was starving,' she said. 'Poor old Timmy.' She picked up the bag and tipped some more food into the bowl. Timothy gobbled that up too, then quickly lapped some water to wash it down.

George laughed when she saw he was so full of food his tummy had grown as round as a barrel. She bent down so the dog could lick her face and say thank you for his dinner. She picked him up and cuddled him close. 'Isn't he wonderful?' she said to Joanna.

Joanna stood looking down at the little girl and the dog. 'I hope your father lets him stay here,' she said. 'Otherwise I know someone who's going to have a broken heart.'

'What's this? Who's got a broken heart?' A deep

voice came from the doorway and George's father stood there, frowning. 'I thought I could smell salmon and new potatoes,' he said. 'What are you doing rolling on the floor with that dog, Georgina? Why is he still here?'

George scowled when she heard her father call her Georgina. Then she managed to smile. If she complained about her name it would be bound to put Father in a bad mood, fresh salmon or no fresh salmon.

She quickly explained about asking everyone in the village if they knew who Timothy belonged to and then what PC Moon had said.

'Thirty days!' said George's father, still frowning. 'So where is he going to live in the meantime?'

'We were going to ask you if he could stay here, Quentin,' said his wife from the doorway. She had been upstairs getting changed for dinner and had heard Father and George talking in the kitchen.

'Here!' frowned George's father. 'But what about my work?'

'He'll be ever so good,' said George. 'And I'll keep him quiet, honestly I will.'

'Yap,' said Timothy as if to say, yes, he would be quiet as a mouse when Father was working on one of his important scientific projects in his study.

George's father stared down at the little dog. Timothy was sitting under the table, staring out at him from under his shaggy eyebrows. His tail wagged uncertainly, thump, thump on the floor. He knew that George loved him dearly and that her mother and Joanna thought he was sweet too. But he wasn't at all sure about this towering, dark man who frowned down at him from such a long

way above his head. Maybe he should try to make friends with him? After all, he was the little girl's father, so he couldn't be *that* fearsome, could he?

George's father was just about to speak again when Timothy came out from underneath the table and sat by his feet. Then, tired from all the games he had played with George and from the two long walks to the village, *and* such a huge dinner, the puppy lay down with his head resting on the toe of Father's shiny, brown shoe. He gave a deep, deep sigh, closed his eyes and suddenly fell fast asleep.

George's father did not move. He stood there looking down at Timothy.

'There,' said George. 'He likes you. Now you've *got* to let him stay. After all, Father, we *have* got salmon and new potatoes today *and* apple crumble for pudding.'

'Apple crumble? Mmm!' said George's father, gently removing Timothy's head from his shoe. He went to take a peep in the oven. 'My, my, that does look good, Joanna.'

'Father!' exclaimed George, forgetting to be patient. 'What about Timmy?'

'Timmy?' frowned her father. 'Who's Timmy?'

'The puppy, Quentin, dear,' said his wife patiently. 'George wants to know if we can keep him here until he's claimed.'

George's father frowned and sighed and shook his head impatiently. 'Oh, very well,' he said. 'But if he's a nuisance he goes to the dog rescue home. All right, Georgina?'

'George,' said George, forgetting to say thank you. 'I'm George and he's Timmy.'

'George and Timmy,' laughed her mother. 'The finest pair of scallywags you could ever meet.'

George crouched down and swept the snoozing puppy up into her arms. 'Hear that, Timmy? A fine pair of scallywags!'

The puppy woke up, yawned, then gave her nose a lick. George gave him the tightest hug she had ever given him. Then she looked up at her father with shining eyes. 'Thanks, Father. You've made me so happy!' Then she whispered in Timothy's ear. 'Just you wait, Timmy, you and I are going to have the best scallywag adventures in the whole wide world!'

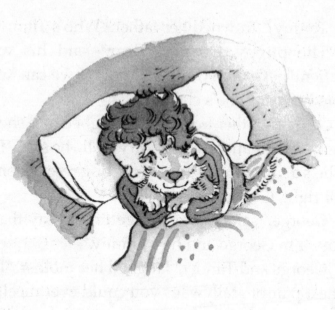

5

George is defiant

'Timmy's going to sit under my chair while we have dinner,' said George as she helped Joanna lay the table in the dining-room.

'Oh no he isn't,' said her father sternly, coming in and sitting in his chair at the head of the table. He spread a snowy white napkin on his lap. 'Dogs *don't* belong in dining-rooms.'

'But where will he go?' asked George in a worried voice.

'He'll have to stay in the kitchen,' said her father firmly.

'But he'll wonder where I am,' protested George, scooping the puppy up into her arms. 'He'll think I've deserted him like those horrible people who left him on the moor.'

'They might not have done it on purpose,' her mother reminded her as she came and took her place at the table. 'He might have wandered off and got lost all by himself. Now do as you're told, George, and put Timmy in the kitchen while we eat.'

'I want him to stay with me,' insisted George stubbornly, standing in the doorway with a fierce frown on her face.

'NOT while we're eating,' said her father, refusing to budge. Once he made up his mind about something, nothing would change it. Exactly like George. 'Tell her will you, Fanny,' he added, looking at George's mother. 'She seems to go deaf when I speak to her.'

'No, I don't,' protested George. She put the

puppy down on the floor and stood with her hands on her hips defiantly. 'And if Timmy is to stay in the kitchen I'll have my dinner in there with him.'

Her father was getting red in the face with anger. His dark eyebrows knitted in a knot over the top of his nose. When he looked like that, fierce and stubborn, he very much resembled George. 'Georgina!' he shouted. 'You really are the most difficult child. Don't argue any more or you'll go to bed without any dinner at all!'

Although George's stomach was rumbling with hunger she felt she would much rather go without food than be parted from her new friend. As usual, though, Mother intervened to pour oil on troubled waters. She picked Timothy up and handed him to Joanna. 'I'm sure you can find Timmy a nice beef bone to chew on while we're eating,' she said in a soothing voice.

'I've got just the thing,' said Joanna, taking the puppy from Mother's hands.

'George, sit down and do as Father says,' insisted her mother. 'Timmy will enjoy having a bone on the kitchen floor, he'd only make a mess on the carpet in here.'

George sighed. 'Oh, all right, then,' she agreed reluctantly, not wanting Timothy to miss a treat. She pulled out her dining-chair with a sulky look on her face, plonked down on it and dragged it back closer to the table. She sat there as stiff as a ramrod, glaring at her father across the table. That's always the trouble with grown-ups, she thought angrily. They spoil everything!

Once Joanna had settled Timothy in the kitchen,

she returned with the salmon on a long, fish-shaped plate. There was a dish of luscious steaming new potatoes sprinkled with parsley and a lovely fresh salad with crisp lettuce and radishes from the garden.

Mother brought in the mayonnaise and sighed as she sat down. By the look on her face George could tell she was thinking that keeping Timothy at Kirrin Cottage for a month would mean more battles than ever between her husband and her daughter.

George finished her meal in record time. 'Please may I get down?' she asked stiffly the very minute she had finished her pudding.

'Yes, of course, dear,' said her mother. 'You'd better go and see how Timmy is getting on with his bone.'

In the kitchen, the puppy was gnawing at a big beef bone underneath the table. George went and sat cross-legged on the floor, watching him. He really was the dearest puppy she had ever seen. She was so lucky to have found him. Then her heart turned over. She loved him so much already that she knew she would love him even more by the time his month at Kirrin Cottage was over. Secretly she hoped that no-one would ever come to claim him. Then she had a very good idea indeed. If she was very, very good during the time Timothy was here, and she trained him to be a well-behaved puppy then Mummy and Father *might* let him stay for ever.

The little girl made up her mind there and then. She would not have any more battles with Father. She would be as good as gold and do exactly as she was told. She knew it was going to be difficult being good for a whole month but somehow or other she really would try to do it.

While her mother and Joanna cleared away the dishes and washed them up, George took Timothy out to play in the garden. She was determined to begin his training straightaway.

First of all she taught him to sit down on command. She had found some crumbled-up pieces of biscuit in her pocket amongst the other things in there. Bits of string, her penknife, an interesting pebble she had found on the beach and some chewing gum wrappers. Every time the puppy sat down she told him he was a good boy and gave him a tiny titbit. The little dog was bright as a button and soon learned exactly what to do.

Then George walked round the garden commanding Timothy to stay at her heel. The puppy was not very good at this and he kept running off to chase leaves that were blowing around in the breeze. Eventually he sat down right smack bang in the middle of one of her mother's flower-beds and gave a huge yawn. He lay down with his nose between his paws and his big brown eyes began to droop. He gave a little sigh and fell straightaway into a doze.

George went to haul the puppy out, hoping that Mummy wouldn't notice some of her flowers had got bent and broken. She tried to straighten them but they kept flopping back over.

'You mustn't tread on the flowers,' she said sternly to Timothy even though he was too sleepy to listen.

Soon it was time for George to go to bed too and her mother came out of the back door calling for her to come in. The little girl picked up the snoozing puppy and carried him gently indoors.

Her mother stroked his soft head. 'He's a very sleepy baby,' she said. 'I've asked Joanna to look in the airing cupboard for an old blanket so he can lay by the stove tonight.'

George looked at her mother in horror. She had already made up her mind that Timothy would sleep at the end of her own bed. She knew he would love her little bedroom with its sloping ceilings and wonderful views of the moor at the back, and side window overlooking the sea. She was going to show him her bookcase full of boys' adventure stories and books on sailing and fishing. 'He's going to sleep with me,' she said. 'He'll be awfully lonely down here.'

'Oh no,' said her mother firmly. 'I definitely won't allow dogs on the beds. Your father would have a fit.'

'But he won't hurt!' cried George. Her heart had sunk right to her toes at the thought of being parted from Timothy again.

Mother shook her head. 'No, George. Dogs have their place and it isn't in dining-rooms or bedrooms.'

'But Mummy...' began George. Then she remembered her vow to be well-behaved and bit her lip. She gave a big sigh. Keeping her temper was going to be *much* more difficult than she had imagined. 'Well,' she said sulkily. 'If he cries all night, Mummy, it will be *your* fault.'

Joanna came into the kitchen with an old pink blanket in her arms. It looked soft and cuddly and George knew Timothy would be warm and cosy by the stove. She took it from Joanna as the housekeeper went to fetch her coat ready to go home.

George laid the blanket by the stove and patted it. 'Come on, Timmy,' she said, biting back tears of disappointment. George almost never cried. She thought it was a soft and babyish thing to do but this time she nearly couldn't help it. She had been so looking forward to having Timothy in her bedroom. She hated dolls and teddy bears and never took anything to bed with her other than her torch and a book and sometimes a length of string to practise fishing knots with. It would be so lovely to have Timothy there.

Timothy gave a little whine and looked up at

her. His big brown eyes seemed to be pleading with her to let him come up to her room. She crouched down and stroked him gently. 'I'm sorry, Timmy, but Mummy says you have to stay here in the kitchen.'

The puppy gave another little whine. He understood every word his new mistress was saying. He had tried so hard to please her and now she was banishing him to the kitchen to stay there in the dark all alone for the whole night. He put his head on one side and softly licked her hand.

George gazed up at her mother, hardly able to stop the tears trickling down her face. She tossed back her dark curls. 'Please, Mummy . . .?'

But her mother was determined. 'I'm sorry, Georgina, if he comes to your room Father will be furious.'

George gave a little snort. *Father* would be furious! Now *she* was furious. Her mother had called her Georgina again just to make matters worse. Everyone was being so *unfair*. She put the puppy firmly on the blanket and waggled her finger at him. 'Stay!' she commanded, her voice cracking with fury and sadness. Then she looked at her mother, her brilliant blue eyes sparkling with tears. 'I won't be able to sleep you know, Mummy. And neither will Timmy. We shall both be tired out and very grumpy tomorrow.' She stamped out of the room and slammed the door behind her.

George stomped all the way up the winding, narrow staircase to her little room right up in the roof of Kirrin Cottage. She stormed over to the window and gazed out at the darkening sky. She could see the last of the sunshine rippling on the little waves that broke over the shore and in the distance the island castle looked dark and mysterious against the orange sky. She sighed and brushed away an impatient tear. She had already broken her promise to herself not to cause any more battles. She was used to arguing with her father but hated to disagree with her mother who was always so kind and gentle. She wanted to run back downstairs and cuddle her and say she was sorry but she was far too obstinate to do that. She just had to stew in her own juice.

George stripped off her shorts and shirt and put

on her striped pyjamas. She crawled in under the bedcovers and lay looking up at the ceiling. She imagined Timothy all alone in the kitchen. He would be scared all by himself. He would be thinking he was lost on the moor again.

George sighed and tossed and turned for what seemed like hours. The house was silent and all she could hear was the distant hoot of an owl and the murmuring song of the sea. Then suddenly the silence was broken by a high-pitched bark and a whine that turned into a howl. Downstairs, Timothy had woken up from a restless doze and wondered where he was. Everything was dark and silent. Where was the little girl who had been so kind to him? Where was the lady who had given him that great big bone?

The puppy gave another sad little whine. He crawled across to the rug and began chewing the corner. Crunch, crunch went his little sharp teeth. He felt better with something to chew on. The rug tasted bitter so he spat out the little ragged bits of wool that had come off in his mouth. He got up and bumbled around in the dark for a while, bumping into the table leg and the chair in front of the window. He felt sad and lost and alone. Then he had an idea. Maybe if he barked again *really* loudly George would hear and come to rescue him.

Upstairs, George heard Timothy barking and whining. Suddenly she could not bear it any more. She grabbed her torch, flung back the covers and ran on tiptoe to her bedroom door. She flung it open and listened. There was no sound from her parents' room.

George ran lightly down the stairs, the torch flashing a beam in front of her. There was a light under Father's study door. Her heart turned over. Father was working on some very important experiment and if the puppy disturbed him he might send him away and she would never see him again. She crept past as quietly as a mouse.

In the kitchen, Timothy was sitting under the table chewing the corner of the rug in between howls and barks. George bent to scoop him into her arms. 'Oh, Timmy, darling, don't worry,' she whispered. 'You can come to my room but you must be very, very quiet.'

The puppy was so overjoyed to see her his tail wagged until it was just a blur. George giggled as he licked her face all over and squirmed with happiness. 'Ssh!' she hissed. 'Now keep quiet!'

Then George noticed the ragged end of the rug and bits of wool all over the place.

'Oh, blow!' she exclaimed in a whisper. 'Now, we *are* in trouble.' She put Timothy down and he ran round and round, his tail still wagging. Then he crouched down and fixed his tiny sharp teeth on the end of George's trouser leg. He growled and shook it as if it was a rat.

'Timmy!' giggled George. 'For goodness sake! This isn't the time to be playing games.'

She managed to prise Timothy's teeth away from her pyjama leg and gazed at the ragged rug. What on earth was she going to do? At last she decided to turn it round so the corner was underneath the table. Hopefully no-one would notice.

After that she quickly swept up the pieces of wool and tipped them into the bin. 'Come on, rascal,' she said to Timothy when everything looked ship-shape again. 'Up to bed, now.'

They were halfway up the stairs when her father's study door opened and the light went on. George quickly clicked off her torch and shrank back against the stairwell. She could hear Father muttering to himself as he made his way past her and along to the bathroom. George put her hand over the puppy's muzzle to stop him making a noise. Her heart was beating so loudly it seemed to echo round the walls and she was afraid Father might hear it and discover her hiding place.

It seemed hours before George's father came out of the bathroom and made his way to his bedroom although it could only have been a matter of minutes. Timothy was as good as gold. Something told him that if he made a noise it could be the end of his stay at Kirrin Cottage.

At last, Father's door closed and the coast was clear. Without daring to switch on her torch George ran the rest of the way up the staircase and into her room. She plonked Timothy on her bed and lay down beside him, giggling when he licked her face. 'Now, Timothy,' she said sternly, 'you be as quiet as a mouse and I'll take you back downstairs before Mummy and Father get up.

With a bit of luck, no-one will ever know you've been here!'

George lay down and pulled the covers over her. Timothy turned round and round, making a little blanket nest next to her. This was doggie heaven. A soft warm quilt and the person he loved most in the world beside him. He wished he could stay here for ever.

6

A surprising headline

In the morning, Timothy awoke first. He had spent a very quiet and comfortable night curled up on George's bed. He had not even had any nightmares about being lost on a cold and windy moor. He sat up, stretched and yawned, then clambered up to the pillows and began licking George's face. The sooner his mistress awoke, the sooner they could start having fun.

George flung her arm up to her face and opened her eyes. She had been dreaming of all the adventures she and Timothy were going to have.

'Hello, Timmy!' she cried, giving the puppy a big hug. 'Did you sleep well?'

'Wurf,' said Timothy, licking her again.

George remembered he was not supposed to be in her bedroom but down in the kitchen beside the stove. She quickly glanced at her bedside clock. It was half past six and no-one else was stirring. The sun was shining through her window and she could hear the cry of the seagulls and the chug of fishing boats as they left the little harbour and sailed out to sea. If she hurried, she could get dressed and take Timothy downstairs before anyone else woke up.

In no time at all, the little girl had flung on her shorts and a jumper and was creeping down to the kitchen. She opened the back door and the puppy ran outside, jumping and hopping, pleased to be out in the fresh air on such a lovely morning.

The paper boy was coming down the lane on

his bicycle. George went to the gate to collect the newspaper.

'Is that your puppy?' asked the boy when he spotted Timothy running up and down the flower-beds and in and out of George's mother's shrubs.

'Well . . . sort of,' said George, explaining that she had found him and that he was staying at Kirrin Cottage for a while.

'Lucky you,' said the boy as he pedalled off. 'I've always wanted a dog.'

'Yes,' called George. 'So have I.' *And now I've got one*, she added to herself.

George decided to take Timothy for a walk before breakfast. She went out of the back gate and along the easy path that led down to Kirrin Bay.

Timothy raced on ahead, his little legs going as fast as they could, his shaggy tail waving like a banner. Every now and then he turned round to make sure George was still following. They walked down the cliff path to the beach. Timothy ran to the water's edge and began barking at the waves as they broke and crunched on the shore.

When the water ran back he dashed after it, then turned and fled as a new wave broke and chased him up the beach.

George laughed to see the little dog having such a lovely time.

They walked along the shore for a little way then George's tummy began to rumble. She decided it was time to go back home for breakfast. Timothy was having such a good time he didn't want to leave. He had found a piece of driftwood and was attacking it, growling and shaking his head like a fierce grown-up dog.

'Come on, Timmy! Heel!' George called but the little dog ignored her. She decided that if she began to walk back he would follow. She strode off back towards the cliff path and as she turned to see if he was coming she thought she saw someone at the far end of the beach. A strange, dark figure with what looked like a very large head was disappearing rapidly round the rocky headland. She frowned. It was very early for someone to be walking along the beach. Who on earth could it be? She hated the thought of anyone else being on her little piece of seashore. She liked

to think it belonged to her and no-one else. There were a few holidaymakers in Kirrin at this time of year but they didn't normally come to Kirrin Bay. George usually had it all to herself, which was just the way she liked it. Maybe it was a fisherman looking for some lost tackle? Or a hiker who had missed the footpath? It seemed very strange that anyone should disappear round the headland. It didn't go anywhere and if you weren't careful you could get cut off by the tide.

But George forgot all about the mysterious figure as Timothy came bounding towards her with the driftwood in his mouth. 'Come on, good boy. We'll come back later,' she said as he reached her. 'You must be starving too and you can't eat driftwood for breakfast!'

By the time the two got back to Kirrin Cottage, Joanna had arrived and was cooking breakfast.

'My, you two are up early,' she said as they hurtled in through the back door. 'Has the little chap had his breakfast?'

'Not yet,' said George, fetching Timothy's bowl and filling it with dog food. 'We're both starving.

What's for my breakfast, Joanna?'

'The usual,' said the housekeeper. 'Bacon, egg, fried bread and tomato.'

'Ummm, lovely,' said George, her mouth watering. She watched Timothy gobbling up his food, then lapping up the saucer of milk Joanna put down for him.

'Was he good during the night?' the housekeeper asked.

'Oh, yes,' said George with a grin. 'Weren't you, Timmy?'

'Wurf,' said Timothy, licking the last of the milk from round his mouth.

George's father came into the kitchen and picked up the newspaper that George had placed on the kitchen table. He went out without speaking. He had forgotten all about Timothy and had not even noticed George and Joanna standing there.

'I can see your father's in the middle of some very important work,' said Joanna with a knowing smile at her employer's absent-mindedness. 'You'd better keep that puppy out of mischief.'

George bent to pick the dog up. 'Oh, I will,' she said. 'I promise.'

When breakfast was ready, George left Timothy in the kitchen. She didn't want to risk any arguments with Father. 'Now don't you start on that rug again,' she whispered, giving the puppy what was left of yesterday's bone. 'Just make do with this for now. After breakfast we'll go and find you some things to play with on the beach.' She gave him a quick hug and went to sit with her mother and father in the breakfast room. Soon Joanna arrived with a big mound of crispy bacon, fried bread, fried eggs and tomatoes all in one warm dish which she placed in the centre of the table.

'Thank you, Joanna,' said George's mother and began serving some on to her husband's plate. He was too absorbed in reading the paper to notice the smell of the delicious food in front of him.

'Breakfast, Quentin!' said his wife in a loud voice.

'Thank you,' mumbled her husband from behind the newspaper.

'Timmy was good last night, wasn't he?' said

George's mother. 'I slept like a log and didn't hear a sound.'

'Yes, he *was* good,' said George, giving a secret sigh of relief. She never told lies and she knew that if her mother had asked any questions about Timothy's whereabouts she would have had to answer them honestly.

'My goodness,' exclaimed her father suddenly. 'Listen to this.' He read out loud from the paper. 'Raid at Kirrin Village Post Office.'

There on the front page was a photograph of

the village shop with Mrs Wood standing outside looking very upset.

'A robbery!' George said excitedly. 'What a thrilling thing to happen in sleepy old Kirrin!'

'It's not thrilling at all, Georgina,' said Father irritably. 'It's terrible. The thieves got away with thousands of pounds.'

George pulled a face. Her father had forgotten *again* that she would only answer to George. He really was quite impossible. She did not reply and turned her head away to look out of the window whistling a little impatient tune under her breath.

'Thousands!' exclaimed George's mother. 'I didn't realize Mrs Wood kept so much money on the premises.'

'Well, she did,' said her husband, continuing with the story. 'The postmistress was in her back sitting-room when a raider burst in,' he read. 'Mrs Wood was held hostage while the place was turned upside down.'

'Oh dear, poor woman!' exclaimed his wife. 'What a dreadful thing to happen!'

'I bet she was scared,' said George, trying to imagine what it would be like to be held hostage.

She felt sure that if anyone tried to hold *her* hostage she would kick and scream until they simply had to let her go.

'Yes, I'm sure she was,' said her mother.

'The thief's motorbike was found crashed in the ditch on the coast road just outside the village,' George's father read on. 'But there was no sign of the robber. He and the cash box have completely disappeared.'

'How exciting!' said George, rubbing her hands together.

'Not exciting, just terrible,' said her father, suddenly folding up the newspaper. 'I don't know what the world is coming to if thieves and villains have to come to a place like this to do their dirty work,' he said, tucking the paper under his arm and standing up. 'Well,' he muttered. 'Better get on.' He turned and disappeared.

'Quentin, you haven't eaten your breakfast!' called his wife. But it was too late. He was already striding towards his study. Then the door banged and there was silence. That would be the last anyone would see of him until lunch-time and maybe not even then. They would just have to

read the rest of the story about the Kirrin robbery
some other time!

7

An exciting find

'What are you going to do with yourself this morning?' George's mother asked her as they helped Joanna clear away the breakfast things.

'I'm playing with Timmy,' said George.

'It's so good for you to have a companion,' said her mother, smiling. 'Although I would much rather it was one of the village girls and not a dog.'

'What's wrong with having a dog as a friend?' asked George, glaring. She hated always being told what was good for her. Children always *knew* what was good for them and they did *not* need grown-ups to tell them.

Her poor mother gave a sigh. 'Nothing, dear, it's just not quite the same, is it?'

'No,' said George fiercely. 'If you want to know, Mummy, it's much better!'

'Very well, dear, if you say so,' her mother said, sighing again. 'And Timmy *is* very sweet. Now run along and play, there's a good girl.'

George took a deep breath. She had promised herself she would not argue with her parents, but being called a good girl was almost too much to bear. She called Timothy and stormed off outside.

In the garden, George showed the puppy her tree-house. It was three planks nailed to a broad branch of the tree. Joanna's husband, William, who sometimes helped Mummy in the garden, had promised to bring George a big wooden box to serve as the living quarters.

'I'm not sure how we're going to get it up there,' said George to Timothy as they both gazed up at the tree. 'But somehow we'll find a way.'

Timothy gave a little bark and ran to the gate then back again. Right at that moment he did not really care about the tree-house. All he wanted was to get back to the bit of driftwood he had reluctantly left behind on the beach earlier that morning.

It was very warm on the beach now the sun was higher. Above George's head, seagulls whirled and dived in the clear blue sky and the sea was so calm there were hardly any waves to break on the shore.

George hummed a little tune to herself as she strode down the narrow path that led to the shore. She was so warm she took off her jumper and tied it round her waist.

Timothy scampered on ahead, his nose close to the ground as he searched for his favourite stick of wood.

He soon found it and came running back to George with it in his mouth. He growled and shook his head as she tried to take it from him.

'Leave, Timothy!' commanded George, trying

to sound stern but all the time giggling because Timothy was so lovely and so funny.

At last, the little dog allowed George to take the stick and she threw it a long way down the beach for him to chase after. Suddenly a flock of seagulls flew in and landed a little way in front of him. He skidded to a halt, his ears pricked in surprise. *Birds*! What fun! He barked and ran towards them as fast as his legs would carry him. They flew off, squawking.

'Timothy!' called George at the top of her voice. 'You're *not* to chase birds!'

Timothy dashed along the sand for a while, splashing in and out of the little seawater puddles left by the tide. Then he sat down, staring up at the departing birds. How dare they fly away! How was a puppy supposed to catch them if they took off into the sky? Looking sulky he turned and ran back to George. She gave a him a quick hug. 'Never mind, Timmy, I'm not really angry with you.' She threw him another stick and he chased after it happily.

They were having such a lovely game, running, jumping, skipping and hopping and so pleased

to be out in the fresh air on such a lovely day, that George hardly noticed they had reached the end of the beach. They were close to the large rocks at the base of the headland, further along than she had ever been before.

Timothy had abandoned his stick and was scrambling around the rocks, hunting in the pools and sniffing everything exciting there was to sniff. George went after him, slipping and sliding across to a shallow pool full of tiny shrimps and fish. Limpets were stuck to the side of the rocks and a scarlet sea-anemone waved its fronds as the water moved to and fro. Timothy was sitting down with his head cocked to one side, watching it intently. What on earth was this strange, colourful creature that was silly enough to live under the water?

'What have you found, Timmy, darling?' asked George when she reached him. 'Ooh, a sea-anemone! Isn't it beautiful!'

They sat watching until Timothy became bored and scrambled away. Soon he had clambered right round the headland and was standing waiting for George to catch up.

'Phew!' said George as she reached him. She had slipped several times and the bottom of her shorts was stained green with seaweed. She stood with her hands on her hips staring at the wide expanse of rocky shore in front of her. 'I've never been this far before, Timmy. We *are* having an exciting time!'

Suddenly George noticed something even more thrilling. Just along from where they were standing was a cave set deep into the cliff. 'Gosh, Timmy, look at that!' she cried. 'Let's go and explore, shall we?'

The little girl's heart drummed with excitement as she and her puppy dashed across to the cave mouth. What a wonderful thing to find. They stood at the entrance, peering into the deep, dark, gloomy interior. She imagined herself and Timothy as brave explorers on the verge of an important and exciting discovery.

'Right, Timmy,' said George, stepping bravely forward. 'Let's go inside, shall we?'

It was even more mysterious and exciting inside the cave than it had looked from the outside. The floor was littered with large boulders and the walls gave off a curious, pinky glow. Pools of water reflected the high, rugged ceiling.

The cave was huge, so huge George could not see the end of it.

'Goodness!' said George, her eyes round with wonder and surprise. 'What brilliant fun, Timmy! This is almost as eerie as my castle.'

'Wuff,' agreed Timothy, sniffing around to find out if he could smell any cave monsters, his plumy tail waving in the air. He gave an excited little bark. There *was* a strange smell here but he could not work out what it was.

George stared at the ceiling, wondering if there were any gulls' nests high up on the rocky ledges. Timothy scampered off towards the gloomy depths of the back of the cave. George hurried after him.

'Timmy! Timmy! Where are you?' called George. The sound of her voice bounced off the walls and came echoing eerily back towards her. She gave a little shiver of excitement. This really was the best fun she had had for ages.

Then, to George's surprise, another sound began to echo around. An odd, ghostly sound,

like a bell ringing from way above her head. It came again, then was followed by a strange banging noise and a weird, echoing squeak and a swishing, swooshing kind of noise that sent shivers down George's spine.

Timothy began barking his head off and running round to try to smell where the noises were coming from. The fur on the back of his neck was standing on end and he was very excited.

'Timmy, come here!' called George, bending down to scoop him up in her arms. Her heart drummed in her chest and she gave another little shiver. This time she felt just a little afraid. 'What was it, Timmy? Was it a ghost?'

Timothy pricked up his ears at the word 'ghost.' He licked the freckles on George's nose. If it was a ghost then he was not a bit scared. His duty was to protect his mistress. He gave another bark and a small whine as George hugged him close. She was quite determined not to be frightened. The noises had probably just been the sea breeze blowing in and out of the cave and the sound of the waves breaking on the rocks. Anyway, she thought to herself bravely, only *girls* get scared.

George and Timothy made their way back out to the cave entrance. George looked round. There was no sign of anything that could have made those strange noises. She really had no idea what it could be.

The tide had come in now and it would not be long before it was impossible to get round the headland back to the Kirrin side of the beach.

'Come on, Timmy!' called George, jumping from rock to rock. 'Let's go and tell Mummy all about the cave . . . and the ghost!'

8

Timothy in trouble

At Kirrin Cottage it was almost lunch-time. George was very pleased as her stomach had been rumbling all the way home. The fresh air and all the excitement had given her an enormous appetite. Finding the cave really was the most thrilling thing to happen.

Joanna was in the kitchen preparing the meal.

'Where's Mummy?' demanded George, going in with Timothy. 'I've got something terrifically exciting to tell her.'

'She's in the lounge with two policemen,' said Joanna. 'So don't you go disturbing them.'

'Policemen!' exclaimed George. 'What do they want Mummy for?'

'They've come about the post office robbery,' said Joanna, busily peeling the potatoes. 'They want to know if we saw anything suspicious that evening.'

'Oh,' said George, taking Timothy's bag of food from the cupboard and putting some into his bowl with a dish of fresh water beside it. 'Well, we didn't.'

'I think that's what your mother's telling them,' said Joanna.

Timothy had just finished gobbling up his food when George's mother and two burly police officers came through into the kitchen.

'This is George,' said her mother, introducing the two officers.

'Hello, son,' said the taller of the two. 'We've been making enquiries about the post office robbery. Did you see any strangers hanging around in the village yesterday?'

George grinned and felt very well-disposed to the policeman who had called her 'son'.

'She's actually my daughter,' said her mother hastily. 'Her real name's Georgina.'

George's smile turned into a scowl as the two policemen laughed.

'You look like a boy to me,' the other, shorter policeman said, eyeing her tousled hair, dirty shorts and scuffed shoes.

'Thank you,' said George haughtily. 'That's just what I *want* to look like. I hate being a girl.'

'That's enough, dear,' said her mother patiently. 'Could you just answer the officer's question? I'm sure they've got better things to do than standing here discussing whether you're a boy or a girl.'

'Sorry, Mummy,' said George, thinking for a moment. 'No, sorry,' she said. 'I didn't see anyone suspicious in the village at all. I wish I had, though, it would have been really thrilling. I was too busy trying to find out who owned Timmy.' She was going to pick the puppy up to show the policemen but the little dog had scampered back into the hall.

'Well,' said the tall officer. 'If any of you remember anything at all perhaps you'd ring the police station. I'm sorry your husband can't be disturbed but maybe you could ask him when he comes out of his study.'

'Yes, certainly, I will,' said George's mother, showing them out. 'I hope Mrs Wood has recovered from the shock of the break-in.'

'Yes, she's fine,' said the officer, 'although she's very worried about . . .' His voice faded as Mother accompanied the policemen to the gate.

'Poor woman,' remarked Joanna. 'I'd be so upset if something like that happened to me.'

'Yes,' said George. 'All that money getting stolen. It was probably some old people's savings.'

'I'm sure it was,' said Joanna, putting the potatoes on to boil.

George hovered by the door. She wished her mother would hurry back, she was dying to tell her about the mysterious and exciting cave.

Suddenly there was a loud bang and a shout. It was Father and he was very annoyed about something.

'That wretched dog!' he shouted. 'Georgina! Come and get this dog of yours immediately.'

George threw Joanna a horrified glance. What on earth had Timothy been up to? She ran out of the kitchen and along the hall. Halfway, she met Timmy hurtling in the opposite direction. He had one of Father's slippers in his mouth and George could see the back of it was all chewed to pieces.

She turned round and ran after him. Timothy had dashed into the kitchen and was hiding beneath the table. Joanna was on her knees trying to shoo him out. Father's slipper, torn and tattered, lay between his front paws. Timothy's tail wagged uncertainly. The tall man's yell had scared him to death. He could not understand what he had done wrong. He was allowed to chew on bits of driftwood. Why was he not allowed to chew this funny-shaped piece of leather he had found at the bottom of the coat-stand?

George crawled under the table and snatched the slipper away. 'Oh, Timmy,' she said quietly. 'I'm afraid you're really in for it now.'

Her father stormed into the kitchen. 'Where's my slipper?' he shouted.

'Here,' said George in a small voice, holding up the chewed article.

'My best pair!' scowled the angry man. 'Ruined!'

'What's happened?' asked George's mother, coming in the back door after seeing the policemen off at the gate. She saw the slipper and her husband's angry face and Timothy hiding under the table. 'Oh, dear. You *are* supposed to be

keeping an eye on him, George.'

'Sorry,' said George. 'Please don't be angry with Timmy, he didn't know it was your slipper.'

Her father had bent down and hauled Timothy out from under the table. George held her breath. If he spotted the chewed rug as well, Timothy would certainly be out on his ear.

'This dog stays outside from now on,' said her father angrily. 'If he chews things he'll have to live in the garden shed where he can't do any damage.'

'He can't,' wailed George. 'He'll hate it outside. He'll be lonely and unhappy . . . please, Father!'

Her father shook his head. 'I said you could keep him here for a month if you trained him to behave himself,' he insisted.

'Quentin,' said George's mother, putting a soothing hand on her irate husband's arm. 'He's only been here a short while. It takes weeks to train a puppy.'

Her husband seemed to calm down a little. 'Yes, I know,' he said. 'But I can't have him indoors destroying things. When you've trained him properly, Georgina, I'll think about letting him into the house again.'

'If *he* has to stay outside then *I* will too,' cried George. 'So there!'

'Oh, no, you will not, young lady,' shouted George's father. 'You'll sit and have your lunch with us. *Then* you may go back outside with your dog.'

When Father was in that kind of mood everyone knew it was no good arguing!

Sulkily, George took Timothy out into the garden. 'Stay here, Timmy,' she said, sitting him down by the back door. 'I promise I won't be long.'

'Wuff,' said Timothy unhappily. He lay down by the step and looked at her from under his shaggy eyebrows. 'Wuff, wuff.'

George went back indoors. She washed her hands and went to sit at the dinner table looking very sulky indeed. She had a dark frown on her brow and her eyes looked like thunder. She almost refused to eat anything but then her hunger got the better of her. Her parents sat in silence. It seemed as if there was a black cloud over the tops of their heads. Secretly George's mother thought it was a storm in a teacup. Puppies always chewed things and they could easily get Quentin another pair of slippers.

While she was eating, George was hatching a plan. She had not even had the chance to tell her parents about the cave. Now it could be her secret. If Timothy wasn't allowed in the house, then she would not live there either. She would pack up a bag and they would both go and live in the cave. There would be nothing for Timothy to chew there that would upset anyone. They would be secret and adventurous cave dwellers and no-one would *ever* see them again!

9

The runaways

As soon as she had finished her meal, George ran
outside to find Timothy. He was sitting by the
back door looking very sorry for himself. She sat
down beside him and quickly whispered her plan
in his ear.

'We'll wait until tonight,' said the little girl. 'The
tide will be out again then and we'll be able to get

to the cave. We'll take lots of food and some warm clothes and live there. We'll have a splendid adventure. All right, Timmy?' She gave the naughty puppy a big hug. 'Never you mind, Timmy, *I* love you dearly even if Father doesn't.'

George stayed outside with her dog until tea-time, then, after tea, she went back outside with him until it was bedtime. Mother brought Timothy's blanket out to her. 'You can make a nice snug bed in the shed for Timmy,' she said, looking at her daughter sorrowfully. 'I'm sorry, George, but you know what Father's like.'

George was so angry and upset she could not speak. She really wanted to put her arms round her mother's waist and say she was sorry and promise to keep an eye on Timmy in future but she was far too proud to do that. Instead she just took the blanket without a word, moved the wheelbarrow to one side, and made a nest with it in the corner of the shed. It was a well-built shed and not at all draughty, so she knew Timothy would not be cold even though she had insisted to Father that he would be. She took the puppy for a last run around the garden before taking him into the shed.

'Sit down on here,' she said, gently patting the blanket nest. Then she added in a whisper, 'I'll be back later so don't worry.'

Timothy watched with big, sad brown eyes as George went out and closed the door behind her. It was already getting dark and a full moon shone like a huge, shiny penny in the navy blue sky. He gave a little whine and lay down with his nose between his paws. This really *was* a strange household. First he slept in the kitchen. Then he was allowed to sleep upstairs with his mistress and *now* he had been banished to the shed. The world of humans was a very strange one indeed.

George refused to say goodnight to anyone at all and stamped up the stairs to bed much earlier than usual. Curled up under the covers she thought of all the ways she could make her father feel sorry for being so unfair and decided running away was the best way of all. Father would be *really* sorry when he never saw her ever again.

Instead of undressing, George had put her pyjamas on over her clothes and now lay under the covers, her heart thumping with excitement. She stayed there, wide-awake, listening to the sound of the sea until her parents were both in bed. Then she crept out of bed to pack her bag. She soon had everything she needed: a blanket from the airing cupboard, two pairs of socks and a thick jacket in case it got cold at night, her torch, some string, a penknife and a box of matches. Down the stairs she went, lugging the bag in her arms. She slipped quietly into the kitchen. There she stuffed the bag to the brim with all the goodies she could find. A packet of biscuits, a huge bag of crisps, some chocolate bars, a jar of jam and some bread, a bottle of fizzy lemonade, and Timmy's bag of puppy food. By now, the bag was so heavy she was not sure she could carry it all the way along to the cave.

'If it's too heavy,' she decided to herself, 'I'll leave some things by the path then go back for them.'

Before she left, George wrote a note to her parents. 'I have run away with Timmy,' she scribbled. 'If he is not allowed in the house then I will not live here either. Please don't worry about

us, we shall be quite safe.' She signed it 'George' without any kisses so they would know how angry and upset she was.

Outside, Timothy was waiting eagerly in the shed. He had heard George creeping about and knew she was coming to rescue him. He jumped up at her as soon as she opened the door.

The little girl held a finger to her lips. Her heart was pounding more than ever. This was another gloriously thrilling adventure. What luck she and Timothy had found the cave, otherwise when she decided to run away she would not have known where to go.

George collected her fishing rod from the back of the shed then, together, the two runaways tiptoed out of the back gate and down the narrow path that led to the bay. The full moon made the night almost as bright as day as the two small figures hurried along. The tide was on its way out and it was not long before George and Timothy were clambering over the rocks to the mouth of the cave. George had managed to haul the heavy bag all the way there. She was determined not to be weak and silly. It was nothing to a brave cave-dweller to have to carry a heavy bag such a long way.

Past the wet floor of the smaller cave they went, making their way through the passage to the larger cave at the back.

George soon found a suitable place and dumped the bag down on the rocks. Timothy was running around excitedly. This was the fourth place he was to sleep in two days. What an exciting life for a small dog!

When she had made camp, George sat down

with Timothy beside her. She listened for a moment just in case the ghostly noises came again. Although she was only a little bit afraid she hoped there would not be any peculiar noises in the dark of the night.

All George could hear, though, was the pounding of the waves on the rocks and a small whistle now and then as the night breeze blew in the entrance and out again.

'Here you are, Timmy,' she said, giving the puppy a whole chocolate cream biscuit all to himself. A rather strange midnight feast but simply gorgeous when you have it in a secret cave. 'I'll catch some fish in the morning and we can make a fire and cook them for lunch,' added George, her mouth watering at the thought.

'Wurf,' said Timothy, thinking that sounded great fun.

Between them they polished off the biscuits and the big bag of crisps. Timothy settled down beside George and gave a huge puppy yawn. He had had so many adventures he was very tired and his tummy was very full. Soon he gave a big sigh and began to doze.

George settled herself comfortably beside a big rock and lay down next to him. Her eyes began to close. She could hardly wait for morning to come. After she had caught some fish she would try to find some dry driftwood at the back of the cave to make a fire. What fun they were going to have!

She had not been dozing for long when she suddenly heard Timothy give a low growl. He sat bolt upright, his ears pricked and the fur on the back of his neck standing on end. George sat up too, straining her eyes in the darkness.

'What's up, Timmy?' she whispered. 'What have you heard? Is it that funny ghost again?'

Timothy's growls were really fierce for such a small puppy. All at once George saw what had disturbed him. A tall, dark figure was standing at the entrance to the cave. Its outline was black against the moonlit sky. George put her hand on Timothy's neck and drew him back behind the big rock.

'Don't growl, Timmy, darling,' she hissed.

The little dog always knew what George was saying so he stopped at once. He crouched, quivering with anger. Who on earth was snooping around their secret cave in the middle of the night? How dare they disturb them!

George was very worried. Surely it couldn't be Father hunting for her? They had left both her parents fast asleep and they would not discover that she had run away until the morning.

Timothy was still shaking and could not help giving another ferocious growl so George put her hand gently over his muzzle. 'Ssh!' she hissed. Her heart was beating loudly and she felt quite as frightened as she had ever been in her life.

They watched as the dark figure began to make its way towards them. Suddenly a light flashed as the intruder snapped on a powerful torch and shone the beam all around. It lit up the way into the larger cave where George and Timothy were hiding. George shrank back even further, trying to make herself as small as possible.

As the figure came closer, she could see it was a burly man dressed in a black leather jacket. He had a shock of black hair and thick eyebrows that met together in the middle. He carried something

under his arm but George could not make out what it was.

Suddenly Timothy could not contain himself any longer. He did not like this strange, dark figure who was trespassing in his cave. His mistress might be in danger and he knew he had to protect her. He simply *had* to bark and bark until he scared the man away.

The puppy was just about to lunge forward when a strange sound came from above. A whistling, ringing sound and a loud swoosh and whoosh in the darkness of the cave roof. The figure gave a loud exclamation of fear and dropped the torch. The light went out and the whole cave was plunged into sudden and utter darkness!

Timothy was so surprised that he forgot he was going to bark and sat back down beside George and allowed her to put her hand over his muzzle once more. Then the ghostly sound came again, echoing round the cave walls and up to the ceiling.

George heard the man swear as he felt around for the torch in the darkness. He found it and tried to click it on but it had hit a rock and the switch was broken. Suddenly there was a louder ringing sound and a louder swoosh and the man gave a cry and began waving his arms around his head. Then he turned and ran back the way he had come as fast as his long legs would carry him. George heard him swearing and shouting as he scrambled over the rocks and disappeared. Then everything went quiet.

Whatever ghostly presence had scared the sinister figure away had now completely disappeared.

'Phew!' said George, giving a huge sigh of relief. 'Thanks goodness he's gone. He didn't look a nice sort of person at all.' She let go of Timothy and he ran around sniffing. He came back to George and deposited something at her feet. It was the intruder's torch, well and truly broken.

George hardly slept at all after that. The appearance of the dark figure *and* the ghostly noises had been pretty terrifying. Even though she and Timothy settled back down on the blanket and covered themselves with her jacket she found it hard to stop thinking about it.

Who or what was making those strange, ghostly noises? She couldn't help giving a little shiver when she remembered them.

More mysterious still, who could the sinister-looking figure *be* and why had he come to this remote and secret cave in the middle of the night?

10

Timmy finds treasure

It was very early indeed when George and Timothy woke up from a restless doze. At first, the little girl wondered where she was. She could hear the sound of the sea much louder than she could from her bedroom up in the roof at Kirrin Cottage. She could feel the salty breeze blowing on her face.

George sat up suddenly. Of course! She had run away with Timothy and they were secret cave-dwellers!

But where *was* Timothy? He had completely disappeared.

George jumped to her feet. 'Timmy! Timmy! Where are you?' she called loudly.

She heard an answering bark right from the back of the cave. It was rather gloomy and mysterious back there. There was a damp feeling in the air that sent shivers down George's spine. She was glad she had made her bed closer to the entrance.

Timothy was behind a rock digging like mad. Showers of sand and shingle flew up in the air as the puppy's claws dug deeply into the ground.

When George reached him he gazed up at her for a second or two, panting and smiling, his plumy tail waving to and fro. Then he put his shaggy head down and began digging again.

'Timmy! What *have* you found?' exclaimed George, kneeling down beside him.

She saw what the puppy had uncovered. It was a large tin box. Written on the side in black letters were the words 'Cash Box – Property of the Post Office'.

George gave a surprised gasp. What on earth was such a thing doing at the back of their cave? Then, all at once she realized what it was. It was the cash box that had been stolen from Mrs Wood's post office! The robber had hidden it here!

'Timmy!' exclaimed the little girl excitedly. 'We've found the stolen money . . . Oh!' George's hand flew to her mouth as she realized something else. 'That man must have been the robber coming to get his loot! When he crashed his motorbike after the robbery he must have run here and hidden the tin.'

'Woof!' said Timothy, agreeing with his mistress as usual.

George felt so excited she stood up and ran around the cave jumping and laughing with delight. 'We're so clever to have found it, aren't we, Tim?'

'Wuff,' said Timothy, still busily digging even though the cash tin was completely exposed by now. 'Wuff, wuff,' he added as if to say, 'Yes, we most certainly are!'

George came back and grasped hold of the tin. She heaved it out of the hole then sat back on her heels. 'Well done, Timmy! You're a hero!' She gave him a big hug. 'We'd better go home and tell Mummy and Father,' she added, forgetting her parents were not supposed to be seeing her and Timothy ever again.

Before they left, the two adventurers dragged the heavy tin to a new hiding place.

'If the robber comes back for it, he won't be able to find it,' panted George when the tin was well and truly wedged behind a rock and she had covered up the grooves it had made in the sand. 'Those ghostly noises in the dark scared him away but he's bound to come back in daylight,' she added.

When they reached the mouth of the cave they saw the tide was still high and it wasn't possible to get around the rocks. George watched the waves breaking in plumes of foamy white with dismay.

'We'll have to wait a while, Timmy,' she said. Then a rumbling tummy reminded her they had not had their breakfast. 'Never mind. We'll have a picnic first. If *we* can't get out, then the robber can't get *in*, can he?'

'Wurf,' said Timothy, pleased they were going to eat before they hurried back to Kirrin Cottage. After all, digging made a puppy very hungry indeed!

By now, the sun had risen and it was another lovely blue day with just a hint of cotton-wool clouds drifting lazily past.

George perched on the rocks close to the cave entrance, dangling her bare feet in one of the warm pools. She was eating slices of bread spread with jam, biscuits and crisps and drinking lemonade. This was heaven!

George had forgotten to bring a cup so she drank the lemonade straight from the bottle. It tasted much better that way. She hadn't remembered to bring a bowl for Timothy either so she found a large, flat rock with a hollow in the centre. Timothy thought it made a lovely dog bowl even if it did make the food taste a little salty.

'Isn't this exciting!' exclaimed George, her blue eyes glowing with excitement. 'I wish we could stay here for ever.' Then she gave another sigh. 'I suppose everyone will have to know our secret now we've found the stolen money. Oh well, perhaps when Father hears how clever you've been, Timmy, he'll let you back into the house and we shan't need to be cave-dwellers after all. Even though it would have been terrific!'

Timothy gave a small bark and licked her nose. He liked it here but it was definitely more comfortable sleeping on his mistress's bed. After all, that was a secret too, wasn't it?

By the time they had finished their picnic breakfast, the tide had receded far enough for them to clamber across the rocks and run home.

At Kirrin Cottage, Father was in his study and Mother had gone out shopping. Joanna was in the kitchen washing up the breakfast things.

'Your mother said you were to have breakfast in here when you came back from your walk,' said Joanna as George and Timothy hurtled in the back door. 'And she said to warn you that your father was not to be disturbed.'

'Oh, blow!' exclaimed George, completely forgetting for a minute that she had left a note telling them she had run away. Then she remembered it and saw with a sigh of relief that it was lying under the chair by the stove. It must have blown off the table when someone opened the back door so no-one had seen it. Mummy must have thought she had simply taken Timmy out for an early walk.

'When will Mummy be back?' asked George, going to pick up the note and screwing it up and throwing it in the fire. 'I've got something awfully important to tell her.'

'She's gone shopping and to have morning coffee with some new people in the village,' replied the housekeeper. 'I don't know when she'll be back, I'm afraid.'

'But Joanna!' exclaimed George. 'We've found the money stolen from the post office. I've simply got to tell her!'

Joanna laughed. 'Oh, George, you are funny. You're having such a lovely time playing pretend games with that puppy. I'm so glad you found him, you know. I always thought you were such a lonely little girl . . .'

'But it's true,' insisted George. 'We're not making it up!'

Joanna gave another smile and bent down to stroke Timothy. 'What would you like for your breakfast, little dog? Would you like some toast for a change?'

George gave a little snort of annoyance. 'Well, if you won't believe me I'll jolly well have to go and find someone who does!' she said angrily. 'Come on, Timmy!'

Timothy followed her outside looking a little disappointed at not being allowed to have two breakfasts.

George went to sit on her garden swing to think things out. Sitting on a swing out in the fresh sea air often helped you think if you had a great problem to solve.

'It's no good disturbing Father,' said George, knowing he hated disobedience. 'He'll be terribly cross and won't listen to a thing we've got to say.'

'Wurf,' said Timothy, agreeing with her.

'And waiting for Mummy is just wasting time,' said George.

Timothy didn't seem to hear what she had said this time. He ran into the garden shed and grabbed hold of the corner of the blanket. He was bored with talking and wanted to play a game. He pulled the blanket out of the door, growling and shaking it.

George jumped off the swing. 'Timmy, there's no time for games, we've got terribly important things to think about!' she cried.

'Grrr,' growled Timothy, shaking the blanket even harder.

George ran to rescue it from his sharp little teeth. It was an old blanket but even so Mummy wouldn't be very pleased if it got ripped.

The more George pulled at the blanket though, the more the puppy thought it was a wonderful game. At last she managed to get it away from him, but not before the corner was torn and tattered. She folded it up with the tear inside and took it back into the shed. She hoped Timothy wouldn't have to sleep on it any more when Father heard how clever and brave he had been but she had better put it somewhere safe, just in case.

In the shed, George's eye fell upon the wheelbarrow. Suddenly the little girl's face brightened and a huge grin spread across her face. A marvellous idea had just come into her head.

'Timmy!' she called as the puppy ran off to find something else to play with. 'Come here, I've just had the most thrilling idea! We'll take the wheelbarrow and fetch the cash tin back here. Then everyone will *have* to believe we've found it, won't they, darling Timmy?'

'Wuff,' said Timothy happily. *Another* run round the bay! Living here with George was the best thing that ever happened to a dog!

George quickly wheeled the barrow through the gate. Along the narrow path to the cove they went, down the slope to the shore.

Timothy gambolled on ahead. Once or twice he ran back, biting and barking at the squeaky wheel of the barrow. He was practising being a fierce, grown-up dog protecting his mistress from things that made strange noises. He wished he had been able to bite the strange creature that had made those noises in the cave but he hadn't been able to see it anywhere.

George giggled at the puppy's antics. 'Careful, Timmy,' she cried. 'You'll get run over!'

It was very hard to push the barrow across the wet sand. Once or twice the wheel got stuck and Timothy barked encouragement as George pulled and pushed and heaved.

By the time they reached the rocky headland, the tide was a long way out. George dragged the heavy barrow from one rock to another and at last they were at the cave entrance.

George stopped, looking inside warily for new footprints in the sand. Then she heaved a sigh of relief. 'No-one's been here since we left, Tim,' she said. 'So the robber hasn't been back yet. We'd better get a move on though, he could appear at any minute.'

Timothy ran to the back of the cave just to make sure the tin was still in its new hiding place. He soon found it and stood guard while George brought the barrow round.

'Phew, Timmy,' panted George. 'This is very hard work.' She was just about to heave the heavy tin up into the wheelbarrow when there was a sound from the back of the cave. George almost jumped out of her skin as the strange noise echoed round the walls.

'Oh, blow!' she whispered to Timothy, her heart pounding like a drum. 'It's that wretched ghost again!'

Timothy was listening with his little head

cocked to one side. Then suddenly he gave a most furious bark. He had had enough of this strange noise scaring his mistress. He really had to do something about it.

The little dog ran around the cave barking angrily and very fiercely. He would not let any silly old ghost interfere with their adventure.

'That's right, Timmy,' called George bravely, her heart beating like a drum. 'You scare it away!'

The noise went on and then it began to change. It started to sound like someone's shrill voice. George felt a tingle of fear. Was

there a *person* in the cave trying to scare them off? Maybe the robber had returned after all. Was he trying to scare them away so they wouldn't identify him?

'Come on, Timmy,' called George with a shivery feeling going down her spine. 'Let's put the tin in the wheelbarrow and get home as fast as we can!'

By the time they were over the rocks and half-way home George began to think she had been rather silly. There could not possibly be such a thing as a ghost. If it had been the robber, they would have seen his footprints. Whoever, or *what*ever had been making those horrid sounds had only done it to scare them. As they got closer to home, it didn't seem so important. The really vital thing was to get their exciting find back to the house as soon as possible.

'What a surprise Mummy and Father are going to have when they see what we've got, Timmy darling!' said George with glee. 'I simply can't wait to see their faces when we turn up with the stolen goods, can you?'

'Wuff!' Timothy said, running on ahead. 'Wuff, wuff!!'

11

A plan to catch a thief

George's mother was just returning with a basket full of groceries over her arm when she spotted George trundling the wheelbarrow towards her, Timothy scampering by her side.

'George!' she called, waiting by the gate. 'What on earth are you doing? And look at you, you're wet and absolutely filthy!'

When George reached her she blurted out the whole story without even taking a breath.

'And here it is, Mummy,' said the little girl triumphantly, showing her mother the cash box. 'Don't you think we're awfully clever?'

Her mother was quite taken aback. 'Are you sure this is the stolen money?' she said, gazing at the tin.

'Oh Mummy, what else can it be?' asked George.

'Well,' said her mother. 'We had better tell your father at once.' She carried her basket into the kitchen then came back out to help George carry the tin indoors. It was very heavy, full of silver and bronze coins as well as notes and important documents.

They dumped it on the kitchen table. Joanna looked very surprised. 'What on earth have you got there?' she asked.

'The post office cash tin,' said George. 'I told you we'd found it.'

'Well, well,' said Joanna. 'And I thought you were playing a game.'

'I'll just go and tell Father,' said George's

mother. 'And then we'll phone the police.'

Father came out of his study to see the tin for himself while Mother phoned the police station. It wasn't long before they heard the sound of a police car drawing up outside Kirrin Cottage and there was an urgent knock at the front door. The two police officers who had called before were standing on the doorstep when George went to open it.

'Well, Miss,' said the taller one of the two. 'Your mother tells us you *have* been having an adventure.'

George gave them a great big grin. 'And Timmy,' she said. 'He's the real hero, not me.'

They all went into the front room to hear George's story. Father was so surprised when he heard what she had to say that he did not even think to shoo Timothy outside. The puppy sat quietly beside George as she told everyone about the cave and the treasure and the ghost. The puppy thought perhaps if he was very quiet, and very good, the tall man called Father might let him stay indoors for ever.

'Ghost!' exclaimed Father when George told

them about the strange noises. 'Don't be silly, Georgina, you know there's no such thing.'

'Well, *something* was making those noises,' insisted George, annoyed she had been called by her full name. 'We didn't imagine it, did we, Timmy?'

'Woof,' said Timothy very softly indeed.

'I'll just go and ring Mrs Wood to come and identify the cash box,' said one of the policemen. 'Then we'll take a full description of the robber from your daughter so we can send it out to all our police stations.'

'Aren't you going to try to catch the thief?' asked George.

'Yes, of course we are,' said the tall officer. 'He'll be going back to the cave to fetch the loot, I'm sure.'

'And we can lie in wait for him,' said George excitedly.

'Wuff, wuff,' said Timothy.

'Yes,' said the policeman, grinning. 'He'll get more than he bargained for when *we* nab him, that's for sure.'

'May we come too?' asked George eagerly.

'After all, we did find the tin.'

'Oh . . . I'm not sure about that,' said her mother dubiously.

'Oh, please, Mummy,' said George.

'Well, I don't think it will do any harm,' said the policeman kindly. 'You'll need to show us the cave anyway.'

'Oh, thanks,' said George, her eyes shining. 'This is going to be thrilling, Timmy, don't you think?'

'Wuff, wuff,' said Timothy. He couldn't wait to get back to the cave to bark at that strange ghost again. And there was nothing he'd like better than to get hold of the robber's trousers and tear them to bits.

'The sooner we get along there, the better,' said the other policeman.

'Yes, said George. 'The tide will be coming in again soon so he's bound to come. If he doesn't, he'll have to wait hours before he can get into the cave again. Then it will be getting dark and I bet he'll be too scared the ghost might come again.'

'And perhaps we can solve that mystery too while we're there,' said the other policeman, smiling at George.

* * *

George's parents waited for Mrs Wood while the two police officers followed her and Timothy outside and back along the path to the beach. George pointed out where she had first seen the robber, then took the policemen round the headland and into the cave. Timothy capered on inside, running to show the policemen where he had dug up the tin.

'Don't you think Timmy's terribly clever?' asked George proudly.

'I do indeed,' said the tall policeman. 'He would make a terrific police dog.'

'Oh no,' George said as the puppy scampered back towards them. She picked him up and hugged him close. 'If no-one claims him I'm hoping Father will let me keep him for ever.'

'After this episode I should think that's very likely,' said the shorter man with a grin. 'I know I would if you were my little girl.'

They crouched down behind one of the big boulders and waited for the thief to come back. George felt sure he would have recovered from his fright by now and would soon be on the trail of his loot once more.

'No sign of that ghost of yours,' said the tall policeman in a low whisper, looking up to the high ceiling of the cave.

'It might make a noise at any time,' whispered George. 'Mightn't it, Timmy?'

Timothy whined in agreement. He could not wait for the ghost to start so he could have a jolly good bark at it.

It wasn't long before Timothy's hackles went up and he gave a low growl. He had heard the crunch and thump of footsteps round the rocks long before anyone else.

'Ssh,' hissed George, her hand on his muzzle. She turned to the policemen, her heart thumping. She could feel Timothy quivering with excitement beneath her hand. 'Someone's coming!'

Sure enough, a dark figure in a black leather jacket was outlined in the cave entrance. Everyone drew back even further into their hiding places. The policemen wanted to witness the robber hunting for the stolen money before they jumped out and arrested him.

George hardly dared to breathe as the man made his way directly towards them. He walked around the rocks to the place where he had buried the tin. He stood there for a moment with a puzzled frown on his face. He knelt down, staring at the hole where the cash tin had been. Then he began digging frantically with his bare hands and swearing in a very loud voice indeed.

This was enough for the policemen. They both gave a shout and jumped out from their hiding place.

'That's enough, my man,' shouted the tall officer. 'You're coming with us!'

The robber gave them a shocked and startled glance, then leapt to his feet and ran back to the cave entrance as fast as he could, with the policemen in hot pursuit.

George released Timothy and he dived after all three men, dodging round the heavy-footed policemen and catching up with the robber. He grasped the hem of the man's trousers in his teeth and began growling and shaking, trying to halt him in his tracks.

'Get off, you lousy dog!' shouted the man,

kicking out at Timothy. But the puppy would not let go. As the man's leg rose in the air, Timothy rose with it, still growling, all four paws off the ground.

George gasped. Timothy could well be injured if the man's kick landed on him. But the puppy was too clever and clung to the man's trouser leg like a limpet until he had to stop trying to run and bend to pull him off.

Just as the man skidded to a halt there was another surprise in store. With a loud squawk and a squeak, something swooped down from a ledge close to the ceiling in a flash of red and green. It landed on the man's head and inflicted a very hard peck on his scalp. He yelled in fear, his arms going like windmills. George gasped in surprise. It was Mrs Wood's parrot from the post office! What on earth was it doing here?

The policemen had got hold of the robber now and were wrestling him to the ground. Timothy let go of his trouser leg and ran back to George with a piece of black material dangling from his mouth. He laid it at her feet then looked up at her grinning, his tongue lolling out. She reached

down and scooped him up in her arms. 'Well done, Timmy!' she cried, smothering him with kisses. 'You're absolutely wonderful! And look, there's our ghost. It was Mrs Wood's parrot all the time!'

As the officers tackled the robber, the parrot flew off again, finally settling on a jagged piece of rock not far above George and Timothy.

'*Ding dong,*' it shrieked. 'Pretty young lady!'

George tried to scowl. Pretty young lady indeed! What an insult! But she was so excited that the robber had been caught she couldn't manage a scowl. So she laughed instead and called out to the parrot. 'Come on, Polly, come to me and I'll take you home to your mistress.'

But the parrot would not come down. It simply stayed up there, muttering and murmuring sadly to itself. George felt quite sorry for the poor creature. It had been lost in the cave for two days and did not know where it was.

By now, her parents and Mrs Wood were hurrying along the shore towards the cave. Mrs Wood had identified the cash box and now they were anxious to see if the thief had been caught.

The policemen passed them, each holding firmly on to one arm of their prisoner. 'We'll take him to the station then come back for your statements,' they told everyone.

Mrs Wood didn't know which event to be the most pleased about. She was very relieved that the money had been found and the robber caught but even more overjoyed that her dear old parrot was safe and sound.

'He escaped when the robber turned everything upside down,' she explained when the parrot was safely sitting on her shoulder squawking and muttering with joy at finding his mistress once again. 'The cage door sprang open and he flew off in fright,' added Mrs Wood. 'I'm so pleased to have him back.'

'Pretty Polly,' the parrot murmured in his mistress's ear. '*Dong, dong*, lady.'

'We thought he was a ghost,' admitted George with a grin. 'We were jolly scared, I can tell you.'

'Well, I think you've been awfully brave,' said her father. 'And my word, that puppy of yours has been surprisingly fearless too!'

'Oh, Father, do you really think so?' cried

George. 'Please could he come back in the house, then? I promise to keep an eye on him.'

Father gave his wife a glance and she smiled and nodded. 'Very well, George,' he said.

'Oh, thank you, Father!' The little girl ran to give her father a great big hug. The tall man hugged her back. Although he was very strict and stern he loved his fierce little daughter with all his heart and admired her bravery and spirit.

'Mind you,' he added. 'If he's naughty again he's out on his ear.'

George looked up at her father. 'Oh, he won't be,' she promised, keeping her fingers crossed behind her back. 'Honestly.'

George and her little dog skipped on ahead of Mother, Father, Mrs Wood and the parrot. 'Maybe Father will even let you stay for *ever* if no-one comes for you,' she said to the puppy when they were out of earshot. 'Oh, Timmy, darling, wouldn't that be thrilling? We could have lots and lots more adventures together.'

'Wurf,' agreed Timothy happily. Staying with George and having lots of exciting adventures would be the very best thing a puppy could ever do!